Learning to Deal with Loss

Loss

Sulaiman and the Tides of Change

Aliya Vaughan

THE ISLAMIC
FOUNDATION

Learning to Deal with Loss – Sulaiman and the Tides of Change

First Published in 2022 by
THE ISLAMIC FOUNDATION

Distributed by
KUBE PUBLISHING LTD
Tel +44 (0)1530 249230
E-mail: info@kubepublishing.com
Website: www.kubepublishing.com

Text copyright © Aliya Vaughan, 2022
Illustration copyright © Rakaiya Azzouz, 2022

All rights reserved. No part of this publication may be
reproduced, stored in a retrieval system, or transmitted in any
form or by any means, electronic, mechanical, photocopying,
recording or otherwise, without the prior permission of the
copyright owner

Author Aliya Vaughan
Illustrator Rakaiya Azzouz
Book design Nasir Cadir

A Cataloguing-in-Publication Data record for this book is
available from the British Library

ISBN: 978-0-86037-806-8
eISBN: 978-0-86037-808-2

Printed Elma Basim,Turkey

Contents

In the Quran, Allah ﷻ says:

**"Indeed, we belong to Allah,
and indeed to Him we will return."**
Surah al-Baqarah 2:156

Note to reader and parents

Learning to deal with loss is a story about a young Muslim boy on holiday with his family when he learns that his grandfather has passed away. Although it is a shock to them all, Sulaiman is particularly upset.

It raises many questions in his mind and evokes turbulent emotions that he has not experienced before. Through it, he learns the Islamic concept of death; how to deal with losses and changes in life and how it is all linked to a greater purpose.

Chapter 1

Scrap metal was scattered across the pavement and into the road. A man's legs lay lifeless under the car.

"Dad, wake up!" Sulaiman pleaded shaking his father's legs with a sense of urgency. *"Please Dad, wake up!"* There was a low moan as the body slowly stirred back to life.

"*Mum wants to know if you've fixed the car yet. She's ready to go.*" His dad quickly scrambled out from under the car onto his feet.

"*I was...er... having trouble changing the oil,*" he muttered sheepishly, rubbing his eyes. Sulaiman smiled knowingly and shook his head. His dad had made a similar excuse when he found him snoring in the kitchen cupboard under the sink. He said the water pipes were difficult to unblock but Sulaiman knew he had nodded off again.

"*Has mum finished packing, then?*" Dad asked.

"*She's just preparing the lunch to take with us,*" Sulaiman nodded excitedly. Dad reached for the new bottle of motor oil, unscrewed the cap and poured it through a funnel into the engine. He glanced up at the window to the flat. He knew he was being watched as the net curtains were twitching. He smiled nervously and waved.

"Quick, give me a hand. Your mum won't be pleased to know I'm not ready." Sulaiman grabbed the tools lying on the ground and packed them away inside the toolbox. He knew exactly where they should go as he would often help his dad fix cars in his garage on the weekends.

"I've changed the tyre and the oil...water's in the radiator. As soon as everything is cleared away, we can get going." Sulaiman was so excited. He loved visiting his grandparents near the coast. It was a long drive on the motorway, but he didn't mind as he would play 'I spy' with Hannah until they had spied everything in the car then fall asleep for the rest of the journey. Sulaiman was startled by a high-pitched squeal as his little brother, Musa, came waddling enthusiastically

towards the car, followed by Hannah and his mum carrying the picnic hamper and bags. They climbed into the car and settled into their seats. Musa squashed his nose flat against the windowpane and watched his dad pack up the last of the tools. He was still squealing and bouncing impatiently in his seat.

"I think that means it's time to go," his dad chuckled, *"I'll get the suitcases."* He snatched up the toolbox and headed back to the flat to collect the rest of their belongings. Sulaiman chased after him to give him a hand.

The journey was surprisingly quick and only one fight broke out in the back of the car with Hannah, which was a world record! The children clapped and cheered with delight as they turned into their grandparents' driveway. They could see grandma at the kitchen window washing up. She waved cheerily, scurried out of view and then re-appeared in the porch to open the front door.

"Helloooo!" she beamed, hugging each of her grandchildren affectionately.

"You must be hungry after your long journey, come inside. We can bring your bags in later." Musa ran to greet all the cuddly toys arranged, as usual, on the end of his bed. Sulaiman and Hannah searched for Grandpa in the back garden. He was sitting on a bench by the pond in his slippers. He was a plump, balding man with a thick band of white hair across the back of his head. Sulaiman joked that even though grandpa wasn't a Muslim, he looked just like one with his white beard and moustache.

"Ahhh! There you are," Grandpa sang happily, *"you're just in time to feed the fish."* Sulaiman and Hannah ran to give their

grandpa a big hug and took the bag of goldfish feed from his hand. They loved being with grandpa in the garden. There were so many fun things to do like catching frogs, hanging bird boxes, searching for sloe worms in the damp, grass cuttings and feeding the fish, of course.

"Oh look! Coco has come to see you," Grandpa announced, smoothing the cat's fluffy fur along its back. Coco jumped onto the patio and stared menacingly at the fish. As they came to the surface to feed, he patted them with his paws through the netting. Sulaiman and Hannah watched the fish gobble up the last of the flakes then ran to wash their hands before dinner. The table in the conservatory had already been arranged for their evening meal. It overlooked a view of green summer meadows that led all the way down to the sea. It was a beautiful evening with a hazy,

orange sunset filling the whole horizon. Everyone sat down to enjoy grandma's delicious homemade cooking.

"*They say it's going to be sunny tomorrow,*" Grandpa chirped, waving his folded newspaper in the air. He liked to keep up to date with the latest weather reports. "*And there's an early low tide, so you can set off after breakfast and make the most of the beach and rock pools.*"

"*Are you coming with us Grandpa?*" Sulaiman asked excitedly. He loved his grandpa's sense of fun and adventure. "*We can make sand boats and get washed away by the sea.*" Grandpa chuckled at the memory.

"*You know I'd love to, but my legs aren't as good as they used to be,*" he admitted sadly. Sulaiman looked disappointed. He remembered how fit and active grandpa used to be before he got sick. They would walk with him for miles across the sand dunes enjoying the views. Now he was only able to walk a short distance and had to be careful not to overdo it. Grandpa used a walking stick normally, but when Sulaiman saw the wheelchair in the porch he guessed his illness must have gotten worse.

"*Not to worry,*" Grandpa reassured him. "*Think of me when you're making sand boats, and we'll do something fun another day.*" Sulaiman smiled weakly. It was hard getting used to such a big change.

"*Who wants a bedtime story?*" Grandpa asked, merrily changing the subject.

"*Meeeeeee!*" All the children cried.

"*Okay, when you've finished your pudding, brush your teeth and put your jammies on, then you can choose a story from the bookshelf.*"

The children loved Grandpa's stories. He would give the characters funny voices and the stories would go on for ages. The children would cosy up under the blankets and as the story trailed to an end, Musa would be fast asleep, and grandpa would be too! It was always a nice way to end the day.

Chapter 2

The following morning Sulaiman and his family decided to go to the beach. They carried their buckets and spades, fishing nets and a bodyboard. Families were already sitting on the sand behind large, colourful windbreaks. A group of children played frisbee and a few young men played volleyball with a colourful, inflatable beach ball. A father and his son wrestled with a kite as it soared high and low in the cool sea breeze and a woman on horseback galloped along the open stretch of sand.

"*Let's go further down the beach,*" Mum suggested, pointing to the quieter end by the cliffs. She didn't like to sit on the busy part of the beach near the cafe and shops. It was too crowded and little Musa could easily get lost. She also knew most holidaymakers could not be bothered to walk that far, which meant there was more room to swim and paddle in the sea without colliding into other swimmers.

"*This is a good place to sit,*" Mum announced, laying her blanket carefully on the sand. She placed the picnic basket on a corner to stop it blowing away in a gust of wind. Dad assembled the tent and hammered the pegs into the sand and weighted them down with heavy stones. The children then ran to explore the rock pools nearby. Sulaiman and Hannah used their fishing nets to catch seaweed and the shrimps and fish hiding under the rocks.

"I've got one, quick get the bucket!" Hannah yelled, holding up her net to show a little fish wriggling in the end of it. Musa squealed with delight as he watched Hannah tip it into a small plastic bucket filled with seawater.

"Look at the crabs! They're fighting!" Sulaiman shouted, pointing to two green armoured beasts locked in battle. Their claws were clasped onto one another. He tried to pick one up, but it pinched his fingers hard.

"Yaaoowww!" Sulaiman cried, flicking the crab high into the air. It flipped upside down onto the sand and waved its claws angrily at him.

"Don't you remember what Grandpa taught

us? You should grab it by the back of its shell," Hannah instructed. She carefully lifted the crab to see if it was hurt. As Sulaiman leaned in to look, Hannah waved its claws near his nose and chased him up and down the beach with it.

Over the years, Grandpa had taught Sulaiman and Hannah the names of all the marine life. Last year they found a starfish clinging under a rock and mermaid's purses were washed up along the strand line. Their strangest find was a headless seal that had washed up on the shore. It was rotting and smelt terrible. Sulaiman and Hannah had to hold their noses to get anywhere near it. The children had a competition to guess how the seal had lost its head. Grandpa even gave a prize for the most outrageous suggestion. Sulaiman won. He imagined a giant octopus had twisted its head off!

This year was the first time Sulaiman would try bodyboarding. Grandpa said that when he was ten years old, he could use the board hanging up in the garage. It was bright yellow with a green and purple streak down the middle.

"I'm going bodyboarding now," Sulaiman announced to his dad, who was building sandcastles with Hannah and Musa.

"Okay, but remember to stay in between those two flags," said his dad, pointing to the large red banners fluttering in the wind. *"The rip tides are dangerous here and you can easily get swept out. You'll need to keep checking that you're swimming in the safer part of the sea."*

Sitting in a patrol car between the flags were two lifeguards. Another lifeguard rode up and down on a beach buggy. Although Sulaiman could swim, he wasn't very experienced at bodyboarding, so he floated on his board in the shallow water for a while and watched the other bodyboarders ride the waves further out. When he was ready, he lay down on his board and began paddling with his arms. Ducking and dipping under the waves, he swam to a calmer patch and then waited until he saw a big wave coming towards him. He quickly turned his board to face the beach and frantically kicked his feet. The wave gracefully swept him up and carried him all the way back to the shore. After riding a few more waves, he decided to brave a larger one coming towards him in the distance. As the wave rose higher, he lifted the end of his board to ride it, but it was ill-timed. The lip of the wave curled over and crashed down on top of him. It rolled him over and over and pounded his body along the sandy gravel below. Sulaiman span around under the water, confused and unsure which direction he was facing. He felt the sand beneath his feet and quickly pushed himself to the surface. As he gasped for breath, he took in a huge mouthful of salty sea water. He coughed uncontrollably and winced as it burned the back of his nose and throat. Steadying his feet, he waited until he got his breath back, and then waded through the waves back to the shore.

"I could have drowned then!" Sulaiman thought to himself. He quickly shook the idea from his head. It was a scary thought and he wanted to enjoy his holiday.

"What happened to you?" Dad asked looking worried. He had seen Sulaiman go under the waves as he played in the sand on the beach.

"Nothing," Sulaiman replied nervously. Water was still streaming down from his nose. *"I just thought I'd come and make sand boats with you."* And that's what he did all

afternoon. Although Sulaiman liked playing in the sand with Hannah and Musa, it felt as though someone was missing. It wasn't the same without grandpa.

Chapter 3

The next day Sulaiman finally got to spend some time with his grandma and grandpa. The weather was warm but windier than the day before, so rather than go to the beach they decided to visit a little fishing village instead.

"Help your grandpa into his wheelchair," Dad told Sulaiman once they had parked the car.

Mum and grandma parked up next to them in another car. He could see Hannah and Musa squabbling in the back. As soon as mum opened the door, the kids scrambled over each other to be the first one out.

"I'll push you," Sulaiman insisted, grabbing the handrails of grandpa's wheelchair he walked briskly down the winding road towards the village harbour.

"Hey Musa! Where are you going?" Mum cried as the toddler broke free from her grip and ran towards the colourful mini windmills blowing in the breeze outside a souvenir shop. Hannah ran to catch up with them, while dad and grandma lagged behind to watch a seagull eating fish and chips out of a discarded paper bag.

Local fishermen were fixing their nets on the decks of boats and trawlers bobbing and swaying on the water. Sulaiman and his grandpa browsed through the gift shops and then stopped to buy ice creams and fudge from the open shutters of a cafe parlour. Musa took one lick of his ice cream but the big, dairy dollop fell from his cone onto the floor. He stood and watched in horror as it melted in the sun on the hot tarmac. With tears streaming down his face, he screamed as loud as his chocolatey mouth would open.

"Shh it's okay! Here, have mine!" Mum insisted, trying to calm him down. She noticed people were staring. When everyone had finished eating their ice cream they continued to amble through the mingling crowds. Suddenly Grandpa noticed a sign at the end of the jetty.

"Oh look, fishing trips!" he pointed. It reminded Sulaiman of his fishing trip last year on the sea in the howling winds. It was a big disaster. He got very wet and seasick

and the only thing he caught was a cold.

"There's speed boat rides too!" Sulaiman announced eagerly.

"Oh... I couldn't read that bit," Grandpa remarked, peering over his half-rimmed spectacles. Before Grandpa could even suggest moving forward, Sulaiman was pushing him at speed in his wheelchair towards the end of the jetty. Grandpa gripped both arms of his chair to stop himself toppling out.

"I take it you want a ride, then?" quipped Grandpa, gritting his teeth as he jolted up and down along the cobblestones. Sulaiman didn't have time to respond. He had noticed there wasn't much of a queue, and he was determined to get there before it got any longer.

"How much is it?" Sulaiman wondered as he read the finer details on the signpost. He

rummaged through his pockets to get to his holiday money.

"*Put your pennies away,*" Grandpa ordered, "*this is my treat.*" He delved into his money bag and handed a crisp paper note to the skipper standing by the boat.

"*Two adults and two children please; Grandma and I will stay behind with Musa.*"

"*You're not staying behind, Grandpa. You're coming with us,*" Sulaiman insisted. "*C'mon Dad, help me.*" They scooped Grandpa up under each arm and marched him towards the boat.

"*But my feet aren't steady on land…they'll be even more wobbly on water!*" he fretted.

"*It's okay, you'll be sitting down,*" Sulaiman reminded him. He and his father helped Grandpa onto the boat and sat either side of him on a plastic seat. Hannah and mum hopped on board to sit in the front. The skipper started the engine and steered the boat into the open water.

"Ready? Hold on tight!" The skipper smiled mischievously. He thrust the boat into gear and released the throttle. Everyone screamed excitedly as the boat propelled up through the water and bumped along the choppy waves with speed. Sulaiman turned to see his mum tugging and wrestling with her hijab in the wind. Grandpa howled as seawater sprayed back into his face and wet his clothes. The thrill of the ride made Grandpa feel like a young man again. As they skimmed across the water, Sulaiman noticed dorsal fins emerging and dipping beneath the waves. The skipper quickly shut off the engine and left the boat to float and drift in the middle of the bay. It was so peaceful. Only the sound of seagulls could be heard overhead and water gently lapping

at the sides of the vessel.

"Look, they're right next to us!" Sulaiman cried as he leaned over the edge. He reached out as far as he could to touch the dolphin's nose with his hand.

"Careful, you'll fall in!" his dad cried, yanking Sulaiman back by his hoodie. Sulaiman watched in wonder as several dolphins leapt gracefully out of the water. In the distance were sea birds huddled on the cliffs and seals were basking in the sun on the rocks below.

"They look like that seal we saw on the beach, don't they Grandpa?" Sulaiman remarked.

"Yes, except they've still got their heads on!" Grandpa chuckled.

Sulaiman wished this feeling would last forever, but as the saying goes 'all good things must come to an end'. It was time to return to the harbour. As the boat glided on the water up to the jetty, the skipper jumped off to tie the rope securely around a post. Sulaiman and his dad leapt onto dry land and helped Grandpa and the others off the boat. Sulaiman ran to tell his grandma and Musa all about the trip. He could still feel his body swaying with the motion of the waves as he ran up the jetty towards them. As Sulaiman chatted with his grandma, his dad lagged behind to answer his phone.

"That was amazing, wasn't it, Dad!" Sulaiman exclaimed turning to get his father's reaction, but it didn't come. He immediately sensed something was wrong as his dad was no longer smiling. Instead, he looked gravely serious and had turned his face away. Mum quickly rushed over to find out what was wrong. Her face grew pale at the news. Sulaiman's heart pounded as he sprinted down the jetty towards them. There

was a sudden outpouring of raw emotion as he learned that his other grandpa, who lived abroad, had passed away. Sulaiman had never experienced a death in the family before and it was hard to take in. His grandparents would visit them every year and he loved them dearly. He remembered all grandpa's stories about when he was raised in the desert among camel breeders. He also remembered going to the watch the quad bike races with his grandpa and learning the importance of praying his five daily prayers on time.

Sulaiman was visibly shocked. Dad gently placed his hand on his son's shoulder, but he pulled away. He grabbed Sulaiman's arm, but Sulaiman struggled free from his grip and ran up the jetty and disappeared into the crowds.

"Sulaiman!" Dad hollered after him, but it was too late. He had gone.

'I'll go look for him,' Dad insisted, reassuring his anxious wife, *"he's probably gone to the stone ship near the lifeboat station.'* And sure enough, that is exactly where he was. When Sulaiman was little he would always play pranks on his parents and hide under one of the stone seats. But this time it wasn't a prank. He just needed somewhere to hide away so no one could see him cry.

"I didn't want to think about dying on holiday," he sobbed quietly to himself, trying to catch his breath. It reminded him of his near drowning incident when he was bodyboarding the day before and it scared him. He curled up tighter into a ball under the bench and pulled on the drawstrings of his hoodie to hide his face and tears. *"Grandpa can't be dead,"* Sulaiman tried to convince himself, *"Dad must have got it wrong."* He couldn't imagine life without his grandpa.

After thinking about it for a moment he felt confused. *"But why would Dad say he died? He wasn't even sick."* His cousin's rabbit was poorly and died last year. He remembered feeling sad, but it was nothing like this. It wasn't the same at all. There were too many unanswered questions swirling around in his head. *"So where is Grandpa now? Where has he gone? Will I ever see him again?"* He wasn't prepared to feel such strong emotions. But then he remembered his auntie saying that the rabbit was old and tired, and it was better returning back to Allah. After they buried the pet in the garden, auntie said its soul would be happier with Allah, free from pain, worry and suffering. *"Was that how Grandpa was feeling now?"*

Chapter 4

Just then, he heard his dad's voice calling him in the distance. He scrambled out from under the seat and ran into the secure arms of his father. As his dad comforted him, he rang Sulaiman's mum to let her know he had been found and was okay.

"Mum's going to take Hannah and Musa home with Grandma. Would you like to go with them?"

Dad asked stroking his son's hair softly.

Sulaiman shrugged anxiously and stuttered. *"I'm not sure… I don't know what I want."* He sobbed loudly. *"Wher…where's Grandpa?"*

"He's waiting for us on the harbour," Dad replied reassuringly. Sulaiman looked at him a little shocked and shaken. His emotions were all over the place and he wasn't thinking straight. His dad had confused him with his answer.

"No, not that grandpa. I mean the other one." Sulaiman choked awkwardly, *"Where is he?"* half wanting to know and yet not really wanting to hear the answer. His dad closed his eyes and sighed heavily. He was also in grief and it was painful to think about.

"Let's walk for a bit," he suggested, steering Sulaiman towards the sandy path leading down to the beach.

"Why did Allah take Grandpa?" asked Sulaiman sounding wounded. "It's not fair! Isn't Allah meant to be kind?" He sniffed, wiping the tears hard from his cheek with his sleeve.

Dad looked deep into Sulaiman's eyes searching for the right response. He understood how his son could see it that way, but he also wanted Sulaiman to realise how Merciful and Loving Allah was.

"Allah sometimes tests our faith by taking away the things we love most," Dad explained as they walked along the shoreline. Sulaiman loved his dad's company, especially when it was just the two of them, but this was a sad occasion and not one he or his father liked very much.

"It's not an easy test when a loved one dies. It can hurt a lot," his father continued, "but we need to turn to Allah during this difficult

time and ask Him for help and patience. Allah (subhana wa ta'ala) will help us through it, and He'll even reward us for relying upon Him."

"We only live in this world for a short time," Dad continued to explain gently. "It's the life in the hereafter that will last forever. We all belong to Allah, and we will all return back to Him eventually. This is a natural part of life."

"But why did Allah have to take Grandpa now? It's spoiled my holiday!" Sulaiman protested. "He was coming to visit us in September. Allah could have taken him after that." Dad smiled weakly as he understood his son's frustration.

"Death doesn't always come with a warning. Allah knows when the time is right, even if it happens when we are on holiday. We should pray for Grandpa and ask Allah to let us see him again in Paradise. But until then, we need to live our lives well, continue to do good deeds and please Allah in everything we do. After all, that's *the whole purpose of life, isn't it?"*

Sulaiman bent down and picked up a few small pebbles from the beach. He then hurled them one by one with all his might out to sea.

"Allah may have taken one grandpa, but we should make the most of your other one while he's still with us," Dad whispered.

Sulaiman glanced up to see his grandpa sitting in his wheelchair on the harbour. He was relieved to see that Sulaiman was safe and no harm had come to him.

The day had finally drawn to an end and many of the holidaymakers had packed up and headed home for the night. The waves were creeping further up the beach like a thief stealing the remaining sand in the bay, and a beautiful orange sunset was dipping slowly into the sea on the horizon. Grandpa shivered as the cool sea breeze stroked the bare skin on his arms. He grabbed his cardigan and hugged it tighter around his shoulders.

As Sulaiman and his dad climbed the harbour steps, Sulaiman hesitated. He feared he had made his grandpa anxious and angry. Grandpa sensed his uneasiness. He stretched out his arms and beckoned Sulaiman to come forward. It was a tense moment and neither of them could find the right words to say. Grandpa glanced over Sulaiman's shoulder and pointed out to sea. Sulaiman turned to follow the direction of his moving finger.

"This beach has changed quite a lot since I was a boy," Grandpa remarked, as though he were referring to a lifelong friend. *"I often wonder what the beach will look like after the winter storms. As the years have gone by, I've seen many changes – in myself as well as the*

coastline." Although Grandpa was smiling, he also appeared sad at the reality that he had finally reached old age.

"The sea reminds me a lot about life. Sometimes it's rough and sometimes it's smooth. But it can also be unpredictable. We never know what's going to happen in life, except for death. That is always certain. It'll happen to all of us one day, so we must make sure we are prepared for it."

Grandpa's wise words echoed the talk Sulaiman already had with his dad as they walked along the beach.

"I'm sorry I made you worry, Grandpa," Sulaiman whispered, slipping his hand in to his grandpa's palm. Grandpa smiled warmly and squeezed Sulaiman's hand tight.

"Are you going to walk me back to the car? I'm starting to get cold," he grimaced with a shiver, *"and I'm sure the goldfishes' tummies*

are rumbling. We're late feeding them tonight."

"*Yeah, my tummy's rumbling too!*" Sulaiman smiled weakly and grabbed the handrails of his grandpa's wheelchair and headed back to the car for home.

Comprehension questions

1. What was dad doing under the car at the beginning of the story?

2. Where was grandma and where was grandpa when Sulaiman and his family first arrived at their house?

3. Name three things the children like to do with grandpa in the garden?

4. What changes made Sulaiman sad in the story?

5. What activities were people doing on the beach?

6. What was being promoted on the poster on the jetty in the harbour?

7. What happened when they came off the boat?

8. How did Sulaiman's dad explain the Islamic understanding of the concept of death?

9. Do you know what your purpose is here on earth?

Ayah & Hadith from the Qur'an and the Sunnah

In the Quran, Allah ﷻ says:

"And I did not create the jinn and mankind except to worship Me."

Surah al-Dhariyat 51:56

The Prophet ﷺ said:

"Make the most of five things before five others [take over]: life before death, health before sickness, free time before becoming busy, youth before old age, and wealth before poverty."

Narrated by Ibn Abbas in the Mustadrak of Hakim & Musnad Imam Ahmad. Sahih

The Prophet ﷺ said:

"The son of Adam will not be dismissed from before his Lord on the Day of Resurrection until he has been questioned about five things: his life and how he spent it, his youth and how he used it, his wealth and how he earned it and how he disposed of it, and how he acted upon what he acquired of knowledge."

Narrated from Ibn Mas'ood
(may Allah be pleased with him)

Al-Tirmidhi, 2422;
classed as hasan by al-Albaani
in Sahih al-Tirmidhi, 1969.